Have fun reading about Marion,
America's Little Miss Patriot!

Little Miss Patriot

NFRW EDITION
National Federation of Republican Women

Illustrated by
Cheryl Shaw Barnes

Written by
Peter W. Barnes

Join the VSP Book Club!
Get free gifts, free books, and special discounts!
Register at www.VSPBooks.com today
and download a free book!

Join our book club and get advance copies of our new books—first editions autographed by our authors! Get discounts on sales of autographed books from our current catalog, such as *Woodrow, the White House Mouse; Nat, Nat, the Nantucket Cat,* and other favorites! Earn opportunities to get free books and gifts!

All club sales conducted through our website. All customer information will be kept confidential and will not be sold or transferred to any other company or organization. Contact us at (800) 441-1949 or e-mail us at mail@VSPBooks.com for more information.

Order our books through your local bookstore or book website by title,
or by calling **1-800-441-1949** or from our website at **www.VSPBooks.com**.

For a brochure, ordering information and author school visit information, e-mail us or write to:

VSP Books
P.O. Box 17011
Alexandria, VA 22302
mail@VSPBooks.com

ISBN 978-1-893622-20-3

Library of Congress Catalog Card Number: 2007933963

10 9 8 7 6 5 4 3 2 1

Printed in the United States of America

Find the elephant hidden in each illustration. Representing strength and intelligence, the elephant is the symbol of the Republican Party, also known as the Grand Old Party or GOP.

www.NFRW.org

Dedication

We wish to dedicate this book to our niece, Andrea Barnes, a future president of the United States!

*We also dedicate it to all of the hard working Republican Women around the nation
who help make America great!*

—P.W.B. and C.S.B.

Acknowledgements

*We wish to acknowledge the support and assistance of Beverly Davis, Utah, NFRW president,
2006-2007; Melanie Sanchez, NFRW political director, and the rest of the team at NFRW
national headquarters in the creation of this book. We also wish to thank Dianne Thompson,
Texas, NFRW past president, 2004-2005, for her support and encouragement.*

—P.W.B. and C.S.B.

Now introducing Marion—her parents call her "Ree"—
As in the word <u>Ree</u>publican, for in this family,
Make no mistake—they dedicate their principles and thinkin'
To the Grand Old Party led by Reagan, Ike and Lincoln!

Mother wants to show the children how to help each other.
Ree helps paint or rake the leaves—keep up now, little brother!
Mother also teaches them responsibility,
And how to make a difference in their community.

Mother is a member of a group extraordinary:
The National Federation of Republican Women – they're legendary!
They help our country many ways, without a boast or brag.
And when they meet, they <u>always</u> pledge allegiance to the flag!

I Pledge
Allegiance
to the Flag of the
United States
of America
and to the Republic
for which it stands,
one Nation under God,
Indivisible, with Liberty
and Justice for All.

They do their work not just because they're loyal friends and pals—
They're solid, patriotic, Yankee Doodle kind of gals!
They love our country and believe, with steadfast resolution,
In the liberties protected by our Constitution!

From Maine to California, Alaska to Florida,
They're unafraid to proudly shout, "God Bless America!"
Ree knows that when she grows up, she'll be pleased to say
That she's a Republican woman, too! It's in her DNA!

Republican women have principles they cherish and hold dear.
One of them is that they honor, celebrate and cheer

The hometown heroes standing by to help or give us aid—
Police officers, firefighters, first responders on parade!

Republican women support the many men and women who
Are in the Army, Navy, Air Force, Marines and Coast Guard, too,

Sending cards and letters, food and presents, so deserving,
To our forces brave and true, wherever they are serving.

Republican women understand a child's education
Helps ensure America remains the greatest nation!
They donate many books to schools to help encourage readers,
For they know, as teachers do, that READERS become LEADERS!

When Republican women meet, there's very little doubt
Of who they are—the way they carry on and stomp and shout!
With patriotic clothes and pins, it's very plain to see
They are the true red, white and blue—the heart of the GOP!

One other group of heroes that Republican women cheer
Are all the devoted teachers who make it their career

To educate our children, and for this, they are adored—
At conventions, they receive the *My Favorite Teacher Award*.

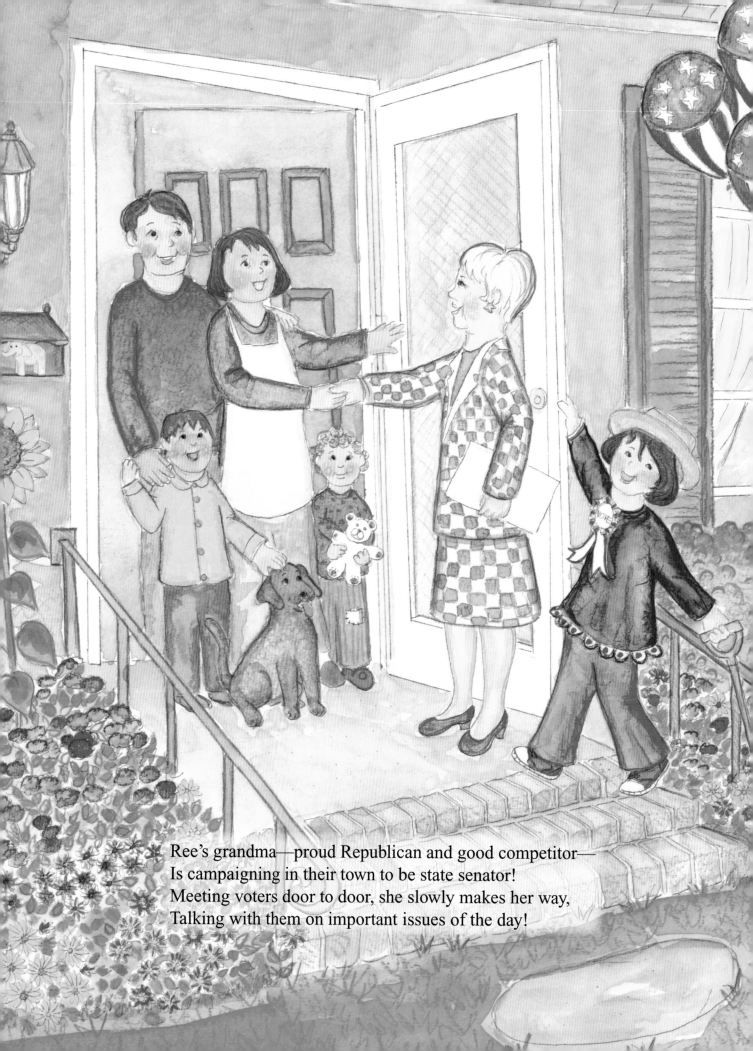

Ree's grandma—proud Republican and good competitor—
Is campaigning in their town to be state senator!
Meeting voters door to door, she slowly makes her way,
Talking with them on important issues of the day!

Voters study candidates, proposals and positions
Carefully, along with referendums and petitions.
On a special day, they meet and then make their selections,
Lining up to cast their votes in what are called "elections."

The right to freely vote is an important guarantee
Within our Constitution, to protect democracy.
Republican women work so hard to make sure people vote.
(When you turn 18 years old, you too can vote, please note!)

We're sure you have no doubt about who won the race that day—
The good Republican, Ree's grandma! Three cheers! Hip-hip, hooray!
Ree was so inspired she decided it would be cool
To run for president of her class at her elementary school!

Join Ree now in her campaign—play our election game:
Rallies, bake sales, meetings, speeches, posters that exclaim
You'll use good principles, beliefs, your heart and hard work, too,
To make a difference and do the very BEST that you can do!

On school election day by 3, every student there had shown up
To stand in line, to wait their turn and vote, just like a grown up!
And once the votes were counted, and then counted once again,
The students learned the winner: Why, of course it's—

Marion!

The students said: "Our school should be the best, and we agree
The candidate most qualified to lead is our friend Ree!"
"Thank you, everyone," said Ree, "For your support today—
I pledge to keep my promises and get working right away!"

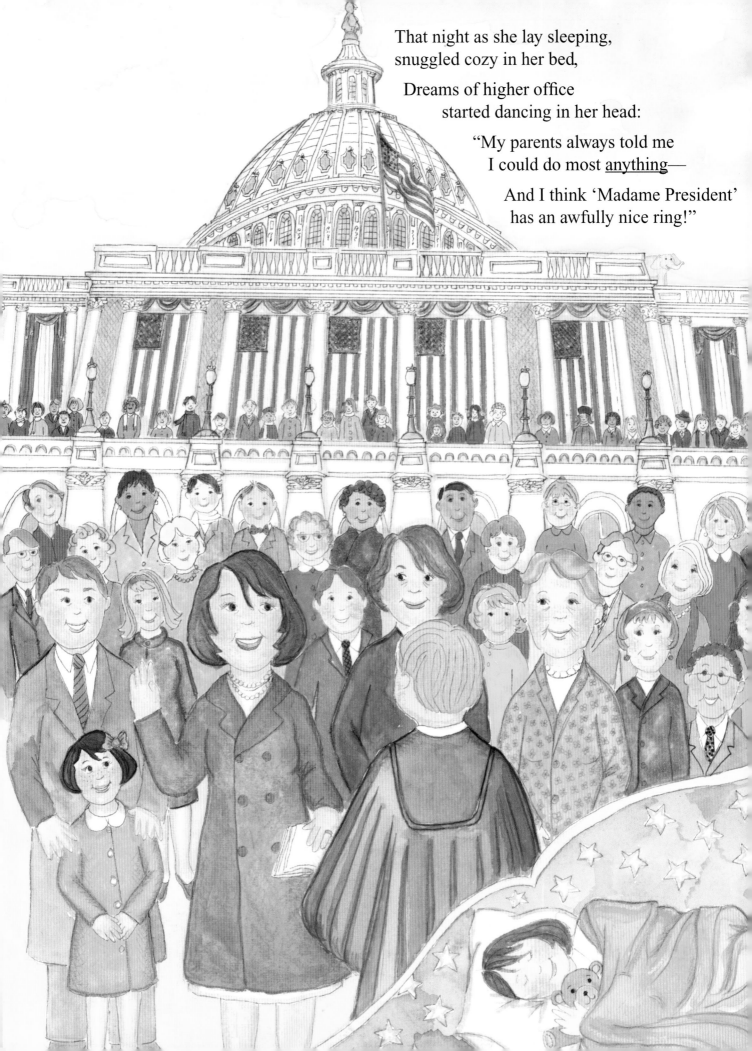

That night as she lay sleeping,
snuggled cozy in her bed,

Dreams of higher office
started dancing in her head:

"My parents always told me
I could do most <u>anything</u>—

And I think 'Madame President'
has an awfully nice ring!"

As a future Republican woman,
it's just the start for Ree

Who will prove to everybody,
just you wait and see,

That in America,
the home of the brave and the free,

A little girl can grow up to be
<u>all</u> that she can be!